THIS

BOOK

BELONGS

TO _Tenisha Diane Brown_

DISNEY'S
SMALL WORLD LIBRARY
HAPPY NEW YEAR, MINNIE!
An Adventure in China

GROLIER ENTERPRISES INC.
DANBURY, CONNECTICUT

Developed by The Walt Disney Company in conjunction with Nancy Hall, Inc.
ISBN: 0-7172-8226-0

"This is going to be the best vacation ever!" thought Minnie. She was riding the train to Beijing, China, to celebrate the Chinese New Year with her friend, Tang. Sitting beside her was a little girl.

"My name is Li-li," said the little girl. "What's yours?"

"Minnie Mouse," said Minnie. "I'm very pleased to meet you. Are you going to Beijing, too?"

"Yes," replied Li-li. "I was visiting my cousins, but now I'm going home for the New Year's holidays. Look!" she said, pointing out the window. "There's the Great Wall!"

Through the window Minnie could see a high stone wall built across the countryside.

"It seems to go on forever!" Minnie said.

"How do you celebrate the New Year?" Minnie asked Li-li.

"Oh, it's lots of fun!" said Li-li. "We celebrate for many days by playing games, eating wonderful food, and giving each other presents." Then her face saddened. "Except I haven't found anything to give my parents yet."

"Why don't you make something for them?" Minnie suggested.

Li-li thought and thought. "I know," she said finally.
"I could make a lion's mask. And my brother could help
me. Then we could perform the Lion's Dance, a special
New Year's dance, together."

"That sounds like a wonderful present for your
parents," said Minnie, smiling.

Before they knew it, the train had arrived in Beijing. "Li-li! Li-li!" her parents called. Li-li stepped off the train and into the arms of her mother and father. Her younger brother, Cheng, gave a playful tug on her braid to show that he was happy to see her, too.

After greeting her family, Li-li presented Minnie with
a map of her city. She had carefully marked all the best
places to visit in Beijing.

When Minnie's friend Tang rushed up to greet her,
Minnie and Li-li said good-bye.

"Have a good New Year," said Minnie.

"Please come visit me if you have time," Li-li called
out. "I marked my house on your map as well!"

The next morning, Li-li woke up very early.

"Wake up, Cheng!" she cried, shaking her brother to wake him. "Today we're going to make a lion's mask for the New Year celebration."

Li-li and Cheng worked all morning, but when they were finished, Cheng began to laugh.

"Our lion's mask wouldn't even scare a rabbit," he said. "Its ears are too big and its whiskers are too short. He looks more like a kitty to me!"

Li-li did not laugh. She was too disappointed.

Minnie also woke up early that morning, and she ate a breakfast of gruel and pickled vegetables with Tang and her family. Before Tang left for work, she lent Minnie her bicycle.

"This is the best way to get around Beijing," Tang told her friend.

Minnie rode Tang's bike down the street of Eternal Peace, past the Great Hall of the People. Then she went to the Imperial Palace Museum. She admired the beautiful red buildings with the golden roofs in the Imperial Gardens.

That afternoon, Minnie bought a jacket that she had
seen in a store window. She was very pleased with it.

"I know just who I want to show this to," she said to
herself.

Minnie found Li-li's house on her map and started off. Before long, she was pedaling down a narrow side street. She stopped when she saw Li-li, who was sitting on her steps looking very sad.

"Hi, Li-li!" said Minnie. "Is something wrong?"

"Minnie!" cried Li-li, her face brightening. "I am so glad to see you!"

Li-li told Minnie all about the lion mask. "The worst part is that Cheng and I can't even figure out the steps to the dance!" she added.

"Let's make a mask together," said Minnie. "We can work on it tomorrow and figure out the dance steps later."

Minnie met Li-li and Cheng at their house the next
day.

"What is the mask supposed to look like?" Minnie
asked.

"Like a growling lion's head," said Li-li.

"Like this," added Cheng, making the scariest face he
could.

"I saw a fierce-looking lion at the Imperial Palace," Minnie said. "Why don't we copy it?"

"Let's go!" said Li-li and Cheng in unison.

On their way, Minnie stopped to watch some people who were doing a kind of slow-motion dance.

"This is how many Chinese people start their day," explained Li-li. "It's an exercise called *t'ai chi*, and it requires a lot of concentration."

Minnie and the children arrived at the Imperial Palace and found the lion standing guard.

Li-li made a sketch of the lion's head, while Cheng had a wonderful time climbing on the other stone statues.

"How's this?" asked Li-li when she was finished with the drawing.

"That's perfect!" said Minnie. "Now let's get everything we need to make the mask."

On their way home they stopped at a store to buy paints and flour to make a papier mâché head. Minnie got some fabric, too.

The three friends began to work as soon as they got home. They shaped the lion's head and then they set it outside to dry. After lunch Li-li and Cheng painted it.

Li-li clapped her hands in excitement. "This lion looks as fierce as the one that guards the Imperial Palace!" she said happily.

Minnie attached the fabric to the lion's neck.

"Put your head under the fabric," Li-li said to Cheng. "Then our lion will have a body, and we can both do the Lion's Dance at the same time!"

"But we still don't know the steps to the dance," said Cheng.

"I know someone who does," said Minnie. "Come with me. We'll go visit Tang's grandmother."

Grandma Peng was delighted to see Minnie and the children. "So you want to learn the Lion's Dance," she said cheerfully. "Wait here. I'll be right back."

When Grandma Peng returned she was carrying a drum. She handed it to Minnie and taught her how to beat out the correct rhythm. Then she slowly taught the children all the steps to the Lion's Dance.

"How can we ever thank you?" said Li-li when it was time to leave. She and Cheng bowed deeply to show their respect.

"Just come back and visit me when you've mastered all the steps," said Grandma Peng. "That's when I'll tell you the legend that goes with the dance."

Minnie and the children practiced the dance every day. They returned to see Grandma Peng the following week.

"I'm so proud of you!" said Grandma Peng after they had performed their dance for her. "Now it is time for you to hear the legend of the lion.

"Every year the Great Lion comes down from the clouds to frighten the people," began Grandma Peng.

"He must be a terrible bully," said Cheng.

"Yes," agreed Grandma. "But if we make loud noises with firecrackers, and wear fierce lion costumes, we can scare him away before he does his evil deeds."

"Is the legend true?" asked Cheng.

"No," replied Li-li. "It's just a story."

"Are you sure?" asked Grandma Peng with a wink.

Finally, New Year's Eve arrived. Li-li and Cheng invited Minnie over to help them decorate their house. They made signs to help bring them good luck in the coming year. Cheng made a sign for his soccer ball that said "Lucky Winner," and Li-li made a sign for her gymnastics' leotard that said "Perfect Balance." There was even a sign that said "Always Full" to place over the rice bin.

When they were finished decorating, Minnie went back to Tang's house for the last meal of the year, the Reunion Dinner.

Cheng and Li-li stayed home to celebrate with their family. After dinner, everyone told riddles and played games. Cheng, Li-li, and all their cousins got small red packets of Lucky Money. Best of all, they were allowed to stay up late to see the fireworks!

On New Year's Day the children were ready to present their gift. Minnie was almost as excited as Li-li and Cheng were.

"We have a surprise for you," Li-li told her parents.

"You do?" they asked. "What can it be?"

"You'll see," replied Cheng mysteriously.

They both ran off to get into their costume. Minnie began to play the drum softly. Then out leaped the lion. As Minnie played louder, the children's steps got bolder. At the end of the dance, the lion reared its head and shook its tail for the last time.

"That was the finest New Year's gift I have ever received!" said Li-li's mother proudly.

"And the best dance I have ever seen!" agreed her father.

"If it weren't for Minnie and Grandma Peng, our gift would not have been so special," explained Li-li.

"Good friends are the most precious gifts of all," said Li-li's father. "You are lucky children, indeed."

Then he brought out some presents. There were gifts for everyone, including Minnie.

"You are right," said Minnie. "We are all lucky to have such good friends."

Did You Know...?

There are many different customs and places that make each country special. Do you remember some of the things below from the story?

The Great Wall of China is the largest structure in the world. Astronauts say it is the only human-built object on Earth that they can see from outer space!

Chinese New Year celebrations last two weeks. A colorful part of the celebrations is the lion dance, which is performed by dancers dressed up in lion costumes. To bring good luck, people hold out cabbages for the lion to grab in its huge mouth as it passes.

Bicycles are the most popular
means of travel in China. People ride
bicycles to work, to do their shopping,
and to go on day trips with their families.

T'ai chi (tie chee) is the favorite morning exercise
of millions of Chinese. It consists of over a hundred
different body movements done in slow motion. Many of
the movements are named after the animals and birds
that they resemble.

Beijing's Imperial Palace lies within the Forbidden
City, which was once home to China's emperors.
Today anyone can visit these fabulous golden buildings,
which are filled with rare art treasures and guarded
by fantastic sculptures of lions, dragons, and other
animals.

Some Chinese clothing is made of silk. Silkworms
produce fine silk fibers, which they spin around
their cocoons. The fibers are made into threads and
then woven into beautiful cloth.

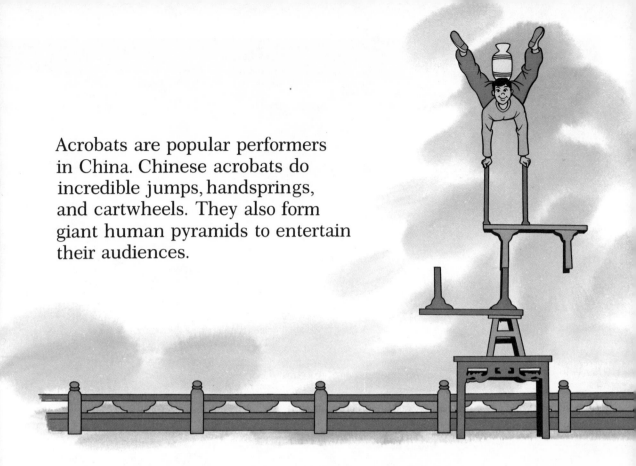

Acrobats are popular performers
in China. Chinese acrobats do
incredible jumps, handsprings,
and cartwheels. They also form
giant human pyramids to entertain
their audiences.

Chinese is the most common language spoken in
China. But Chinese is spoken differently in different
places, often making it impossible for a person in one
region or village to understand someone from another.

Instead of letters the Chinese use little pictures, called
characters, to write their words. There are over 40,000
different characters! The character Tang has drawn
represents the word "tree."

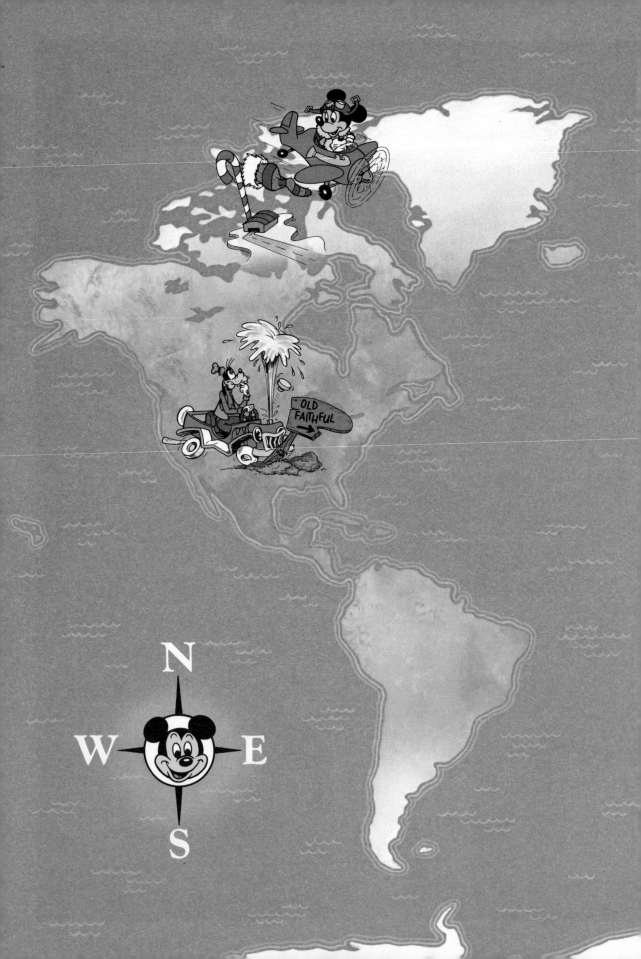